North Pole

To Amanda, Neil, Otis and Leah
~J.S.

For my good friends
Jim and Raechele
~T.W.

LITTLE TIGER PRESS
an imprint of Magi Publications
1 The Coda Centre, 189 Munster Road, London SW6 6AW
www.littletigerpress.com

First Published in Great Britain 2002

Text © Julie Sykes 2002
Illustration © Tim Warnes 2002

ISBN 1 85430 824 6

A CIP catalogue record for this book
is available from the British Library

Printed in Belgium by Proost

2 4 6 8 10 9 7 5 3 1

Careful, Santa!

Julie Sykes   Tim Warnes

LITTLE TIGER PRESS

London

It was Christmas Eve, and
Santa was loading presents
on to his sleigh. Santa's little
mouse was helping too.
WHOOSH!
A gust of wind blew Santa's
beard straight in his face.
"Ho, ho, ho!" he chuckled.
"I can't see what I'm doing!"
"Careful, Santa!" warned
Santa's cat. "You mustn't
lose that sack of presents."

"That would never do!" Santa agreed,
as he carefully stowed everything away.

Santa helped his little mouse climb aboard
the sleigh.
"Hold on tight!" he boomed. "We're off!"
It was a wild and windy night.
"Oooh my!" shouted Santa, as the sleigh
rocked this way and that. Suddenly, the sack
of presents began to move.
"Careful, Santa!" called Santa's little mouse.
"Mind that sack!"

But Santa wasn't quick enough.
The sack slid across the sleigh and toppled overboard.
"Stop!" cried Santa in alarm. "Down, Reindeer, down!
I've lost all the presents!"

The reindeer struggled
against the wind . . .

and landed as gently as they could.

"Careful, Santa!" they shouted, but it was too late . . .

"WHOOPS!" cried Santa, landing on his bottom.

Santa scrambled to his feet.
The presents were scattered far and
wide and he hurried to pick them up.
He didn't notice the frozen pond . . .

"WHEEEEEE!" cried Santa,
as he slid across the ice towards
the duckhouse.

"Careful, Santa!" quacked the ducks.
"You nearly squashed us."
"How awful," said Santa as he gathered
up the presents. "Sorry about that.
Has anyone seen my sack?"

"Here it is!" chattered a squirrel from high in a tree. Santa bravely climbed up, but before he knew it he was well and truly stuck. "Oooh, help!" he cried.

"Careful, Santa!"
called the squirrel.
"I am trying to be careful,"
said Santa, as he struggled
to get free.
    Very, very slowly, Santa
    climbed back down again,
        dropping some presents
        as he went.

In the playground, a few presents were lying
under the swings. Santa put them into his
sack, then he spotted some more on the slide.

"Whoooooosh!" cried Santa, as he whizzed down the slide.
"Careful, Santa, you're going too fast!" warned Santa's cat.
"Eeek! I can't stop!" said Santa, as he zoomed towards
the snowman . . .

"Sorry, Snowman, I didn't mean to bump you," Santa said, as
he dusted himself down and popped the last of the presents
into his sack.

"That's it!" he boomed. "It's time to deliver these presents. Ready, Mouse?" But where was Mouse? Santa couldn't see her anywhere. "Oh dear!" he cried in alarm. "First I lose my sack of presents, and now I've lost my little mouse. This will never do."

The ducks, the squirrel and Santa's cat all crowded round. "Don't worry, Santa!" they chattered. "She can't have gone far. We'll help you look for her."

Everyone looked
for Mouse.
She wasn't in the
duckhouse,

and she wasn't
at the swings.

She wasn't near the slide
or behind the snowman.

Just then, Santa heard a
familiar squeak. He shone
his torch upwards . . .

and there was Mouse, hanging from a branch in
a tree.
"Careful!" warned Santa. "It's far too windy to play
up there. That branch doesn't look too safe to me."

But Mouse wasn't playing. "I'm stuck," she squeaked. "Please get me down!" Quickly, Santa took off his jacket and spread it out on the ground. Everyone gathered round and held the coat like a trampoline. "Hold on tight, everyone, and don't let go!" said Santa.

"Ready, Mouse?
One, two, three . . .
JUMP!"
Mouse jumped and, with a bounce and a plop,
landed safely on Santa's coat.
"Hooray!" cheered Santa. "Thank you, everyone."

It was time to go. Santa and Mouse
hurried aboard their sleigh.
"Reindeer, up, up and away!" cried Santa.
WHOOSH! blew the wind.

"Careful, Santa," called everyone,
as the sleigh rocked this way and that.
"Look after that mouse, and HOLD
ON TIGHT TO THAT SACK!"